W9-CTU-212

AN ULTIMATUM ...

"I thought this was one of the days you were supposed to be at our practice," Will started in. "The coaches were counting on you."

Jo didn't like the way Will and Brian were looking at her. She spun her basketball on her right index finger, trying to strike a casual pose.

"Rehearsal ran late," Jo said. "Nothing I could do about it. I couldn't leave in the middle of a scene, could I?"

Brian stood straddled over the crossbar of his bike with a belligerent look on his face. "If rehearsals run so late all the time," he challenged, "why don't you skip them once in a while?"

"Are you *kidding*?" Jo screeched. "I can't do that. I'd be kicked right out of the play!"

Brian just stared back at her, smiling nastily. Jo knew what he was thinking: *Miss enough practices, and you could be kicked off the Bulls too!*

Don't miss any of the books in

—a slammin', jammin', in-your-face action series
from Bantam Books!

REBOUND!

by
Hank Herman

BANTAM BOOKS
NEW YORK · TORONTO · LONDON · SYDNEY · AUCKLAND

RL 2.6, 007-010

REBOUND!

A Bantam Book / January 1998

Produced by Daniel Weiss Associates, Inc.
33 West 17th Street
New York, NY 10011.

Cover art by Jeff Mangiat.

All rights reserved.

Copyright © 1998 by Daniel Weiss Associates, Inc., and
Hank Herman.

Cover art copyright © 1998 by Daniel Weiss Associates, Inc.
No part of this book may be reproduced or transmitted
in any form or by any means, electronic or mechanical,
including photocopying, recording, or by any information
storage and retrieval system, without permission in
writing from the publisher.
For information address: Bantam Books.

If you purchased this book without a cover you should be aware
that this book is stolen property. It was reported as "unsold and
destroyed" to the publisher and neither the author nor the publisher has
received any payment for this "stripped book."

ISBN: 0-553-48595-4
Published simultaneously in the United States and Canada

Bantam Books are published by Bantam Books, a division of Bantam
Doubleday Dell Publishing Group, Inc. Its trademark, consisting of the
words "Bantam Books" and the portrayal of a rooster, is Registered in U.S.
Patent and Trademark Office and in other countries. Marca Registrada.
Bantam Books, 1540 Broadway, New York, New York 10036.

PRINTED IN THE UNITED STATES OF AMERICA

OPM   0 9 8 7 6 5 4 3 2 1

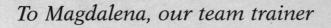

To Magdalena, our team trainer

CHAPTER 1

Jo leaned hard against her brother, determined not to let him use his weight advantage to back her in under the hoop in front of their house.

Otto dribbled with his back to the basket, edging closer, closer, closer. He kept looking back over his shoulder at Jo, an obnoxious grin on his pudgy, freckled face. "Better be ready," he taunted. "Better be ready now. . . ."

"Yeah, I'm ready," Jo shot back. "Ready for *nothing!*"

Jo hated when her older brother gave her warnings before going into his move—just to rub in how unstoppable he was. Maybe this was only a two-on-two game in their driveway, but she never liked losing to Otto. *Never.*

In the midst of Otto's endless dribbling, Jo noticed him cup the ball for a split second in his right palm. He was committing himself to drive to his right! Jo scooted to her left to cut off his path. She moved so quickly that her green baseball cap flew off her head and fell to the driveway.

But the moment Jo shifted her weight, Otto did a beautiful crossover dribble, switching the ball to his left hand. Then he sped to the hoop, making the layup from the left side unchallenged.

"Schooled again!" Otto crowed. "When is my wittle sister gonna learn that my killer crossover is right up there with Tim Hardaway's—and that I can go to my left the way most people can only in their dreams?"

Matt Johnstone and Spider McHale both laughed at Otto's trash talk—even though Spider was Jo's teammate for this game!

Jo fumed. *"Wittle sister"! So Otto's thirteen months older than I am—big deal! Why do I even bother playing with these guys?* she asked herself for the hundredth time. Spider was a tall, gangly kid who always wore a black wool cap, even on a warm, sunny spring afternoon like this one. Matt was short and skinny, with bright red hair that made him look like a lit match. They were her brother's best buddies on the Sampton Slashers—a team that hadn't let Jo try out because she was a girl!

It had worked out for the best, Jo supposed. Eventually she'd made the Branford Bulls, a team from a neighboring town. The kids were a lot nicer, and the Bulls were just as good as the Slashers—if not better.

3

But Jo had never forgiven Otto and his jerky sidekicks for turning her away. And even though she'd proven that she could play basketball as well as any of them, they still always made fun of her as Otto's "wittle sister."

"Loser's out," Otto reminded Jo as he checked the ball for her after his basket. "I think that would be you. . . ."

Jo bit her lip. *I'll get him back,* she promised herself. *Maybe not right this second, but I'll get him back.*

She passed the ball in to Spider, who was positioned just above the white foul line painted on the driveway. Spider, who played forward for the Slashers, was four inches taller than Matt. Using that advantage, he put up an old-fashioned hook shot that the red-haired guard couldn't come close to defending. The ball bounced twice on the rim, then fell off to the left of the hoop.

Otto gathered in the rebound and

shook his head in disbelief. "I haven't seen a shot like that since the days of Kareem," he said mockingly, referring to Kareem Abdul-Jabbar, the Lakers' legendary Hall of Fame center.

That's just like Otto, Jo thought, rolling her eyes. Her brother and his friends had no use for any of the stars who didn't play the game *today.* She could never understand his disrespect for the legends. She was also amazed that Otto was constantly dissing his own teammates—even if Spider happened to be his opponent for the moment.

Otto brought the ball back to the top of the key on the change of possession. Then he began backing Jo into the hoop again.

But though this was the way he'd started a few moments earlier, Jo knew she'd better be ready for something different. *He's going to stop and pop—I know it!* she told herself. *He's going to shoot the turnaround jumper.* She'd played her brother man-to-man often enough to know he didn't like to repeat the same move twice in a row. As for the possibility of his passing, well, *that* was something she knew she didn't have to worry about!

Sure enough, after two more back-to-the-basket dribbles, Otto stopped, pivoted, and jumped.

Jo timed her leap perfectly, jumping just a split second later.

Swat!

"Get outta my house!" Jo yelled gleefully as Spider retrieved the blocked shot just before it squirted into the bushes alongside the Meyersons' driveway. *I love it when my brother eats leather!* she thought. *Sweet revenge!*

She saw Otto holding his wrist, as if he was considering calling a foul, but he thought better of it.

Even Otto wouldn't make a call as lame as that, Jo thought with satisfaction. *That was* all ball—*and everyone could see it!*

Spider threw Jo a bounce pass, then tried to get position under the basket. Jo was way out above the top of the key, maybe thirty feet from the basket. *Nailing a three-pointer would really add insult to injury,* she thought as she considered taking the shot.

Otto, seeing his sister square up, charged at her with fire in his eyes. But before he could get close enough, she'd launched the long bomb.

For a moment Otto looked furious. Then he threw his hands straight up in the air, like a referee indicating a three-point goal.

"Six!" he called out.

Six? Jo wondered what her ridiculous brother was up to *this* time.

"*What* are you talking about?" she asked.

"Well," he said as a mischievous grin stole across his face, "looked to me like you fired that one up with a six-shooter, hey, Annie?" At the word *Annie,* Otto winked at his two buddies.

So that's it! Jo realized. Otto figured he could draw attention away from being burned twice by making fun of her for her new role in *Annie Get Your Gun,* the Sampton Middle School spring play.

"Yeah," Spider chimed in, right on cue. "I guess you can do anything better than us!" He laughed and poked Matt in the chest

Jo rolled her eyes. "Anything You Can Do" was one of the songs she sang as Annie Oakley.

Matt picked up on the ribbing. "You know," he added, "most of the kids think you're in the play because you like to sing. But I know the *real* reason." He rubbed his hands together, enjoying Jo's discomfort. "It's because Duncan Gaines plays Frank Butler, isn't it? For some reason a lot of the girls think that pretty boy's a hunk. And I'll bet Jo's got the hots for him!" He shot a leering grin at Otto and Spider, and all three Slashers burst into hysterics.

Jo felt her face getting warm. This wasn't the first time her brother and his sidekicks had gotten on her about being in the theater production. She'd tried to teach herself not to react to their idiotic teasing, but somehow she couldn't help it.

"Exactly what is it you dummies have against me playing Annie Oakley?" Jo challenged.

Otto gave her a scornful, do-I-really-have-to-explain-this expression. "Come on, sis, either you're a cool basketball player—like us," he replied, glancing around at Spider and Matt, "or you're a wimpy actor in a lame school play with a bunch of losers. That's just how it is." He spun the basketball nonchalantly on his right index finger as he spoke. "Well, which is it?" he pressed, tossing the ball to Jo.

All three—Otto, Matt, and Spider—stared at her, waiting for her response.

For a few seconds Jo spun the ball on her own finger. It was a trick she could do as well as Otto. Then, without warning, she fired the ball hard at Otto's stomach. He grunted, and for a few seconds he was unable to catch his breath. *Serves him right,* Jo thought.

"You guys are a bunch of *jerks!*" she spat, then turned and ran into the kitchen, letting the screen door slam behind her. No way she was going to let any of them see the tears in her eyes.

She heard Otto, who'd recovered

his breath, call after her, "Oh, come on, Sis, we were just yanking your chain."

Jo knew her brother was only pretending to be nice so he wouldn't get in trouble with their parents. She refused to look back. She'd had enough of Otto and his miserable friends for one afternoon.

CHAPTER 2

Jo raced up to the two stone pillars on Mulberry Avenue, made a sharp right turn into Jefferson Park, then darted down the narrow paved path to the blacktop basketball court. She dribbled her basketball expertly the whole time—as if she were on a fast break.

Play rehearsal hadn't lasted too long, and Jo figured if she hurried, she still had a chance to make it to practice on time. She didn't want to be the last one there and have to answer all kinds of questions about where she'd been. She knew how seriously the Bulls took practice.

Oh, man! she thought. The black-top, visible through the trees, already looked pretty full. Even though she was still about a hundred yards from the court, she could make out her teammates easily.

The one with the dark hair, endlessly working on his moves under the basket, was Will Hopwood, the center. The slender forward gliding gracefully around the perimeter was Derek Roberts, the Bulls' best player. Playing one-on-one and trying to outdo each other with their hotdog moves, as usual, were David Danzig and Brian Simmons, best buddies and next-door neighbors.

Jo could also make out a pudgy kid practicing his free throws: Chunky Schwartz, the backup center. The one with the white goggles bombing from long range was Mark Fisher, the second-

13

string guard. And MJ Jordan, who liked to talk more than play, was conferring with Jim Hopwood and Nate Bowman, the two teenage coaches.

So everyone else on the Branford Bulls was there already. She was dead last, just as she'd feared. *Man, juggling play rehearsal and basketball practice is no piece of cake!* Jo thought.

Mark was the first to hear the sound of Jo's basketball. He turned around, pointed at her face—and burst into a loud cackle.

His reaction made Jo freeze. She realized that in her desperate rush to make it to Jefferson on time, she'd forgotten to take off her makeup!

She knew she looked ridiculous as she used the back of her hand to wipe off her lipstick, and she could tell by Mark's grin that he was relishing the situation. The only thing Mark loved more than shooting threes was ragging on his teammates.

"That shade does wonders for you, *dahling*," Mark cooed, pointing to Jo's red lipstick. All the Bulls stopped whatever they'd been doing on the court and gathered around Jo at the edge of the blacktop, curious looks on their faces.

From the time she'd won the starring role in the school play, Jo's intuition had told her she'd be better off keeping the information from the Bulls as long as possible. The teasing she'd gotten from Otto and the Slashers only confirmed that feeling. Now, however, it looked as though she'd have to come out with it.

Jo figured her best defense was to make her admission with some flash. "Our school's putting on *Annie Get Your Gun,*" she said, trying to sound real confident. Then, pretending to take aim with an imaginary rifle, she added, "And *I'm* Annie Oakley!"

She braced herself for hooting, pointing, and wise remarks.

Mark just shrugged. "I'd rather be *Charles* Oakley than Annie Oakley any day," he said. Then he went back to launching his three-point shots. A number of the other Bulls followed him back onto the court.

"Why would you want to have to memorize all those lines, and then get up and say them with the whole school watching?" Will wanted to know. But besides Will's question and similar expressions of curiosity from a few of her other teammates, none of the Bulls made a big fuss the way the Slashers had. As a matter of fact, the coaches and a few of the players found the idea of a theater production kind of intriguing.

"I've never been in a school play," MJ began. "How did you have the nerve to try out for the part in front of all those people?"

After Jo finished telling about the auditions, the set building, the stage-hands—everything that went into the production—Derek, the quietest of the Bulls, nodded solemnly and said, "That's pretty cool."

"You guys have to rehearse much?"

Nate asked in an offhand way as he headed back onto the blacktop, dribbling between his legs.

Jo had been dreading this question. She gulped before answering. "Yeah, kind of," she began timidly. "Starting next week, we'll be rehearsing after school three times a week." The last sentence was delivered very rapidly. Jo was hoping that if she sped through her answer, maybe no one would pay too much attention to what she was saying.

But she could tell her reply didn't get by Jim, who'd been watching Will and Derek go at it one-on-one. He suddenly turned and faced her, eyebrows raised. He didn't say anything, though.

Jo figured now that she'd started, she'd better come out with all of it. "That means I'll be missing three practices a week," she raced on. "And maybe a game here and there, since we have some weekend rehearsals too. And of course the weekend of the play, I'll obviously have to miss our game."

At the mention of missing practices and games, some of her teammates who'd lost interest in the theater conversation now returned to the edge of the blacktop, where Jo was standing.

"You might miss a *game* here and there?" Brian repeated in disbelief. "We're barely at .500 as it is. We need to win every game from here on out!"

"And don't forget what Jim and Nate always tell us," Chunky was quick to add. "No practice, no start."

"Hey, you can't put on a good play without a lot of rehearsals," Jo responded defensively. "Everyone knows that."

Will walked over to Jo and looked down at her. At five foot four, he had about six inches on her, even with her green baseball cap. "What I want to know," he said, "is how you can put some stupid play in front of hoops?"

Will's remark sounded strangely familiar to Jo—and it made her furious.

"You know," she shot back, "you sound more like my obnoxious brother all the time." Though she hadn't intended it, her voice was beginning to rise. "Here, read my lips," she continued. "I want to play basketball. *And* I want to be in the play. Now what part of that didn't you understand?"

She was almost screaming at the end of her question to Will. No wonder her teammates were all staring at her wordlessly.

She slammed her ball down onto the blacktop and caught it as it sprang back up.

"Come on, let's stop talking and play some hoops," she said angrily.

She was beginning to wonder if the Bulls were really that much nicer than the Slashers after all.

CHAPTER 3

Jo couldn't take her eyes off number thirty-seven in the neon orange-and-green Essex uniform, Sky Jones. The tall forward's black skin shone with sweat, and the cut-off T-shirt he wore under his jersey revealed rippling muscles. As if Sky's physique weren't imposing enough, he had lightning bolts shaved into his close-cropped hair!

Sky was poised above the key on the left side of the court. He held the ball out in front of his body in the triple-threat position: ready to pass, drive, or shoot. Jo could see that Derek, who was guarding the Essex star, didn't want to play him too tight, for fear of being burned by a drive. But he also couldn't lay too far off Sky, because the Eagles' forward had a deadly jumper.

Sky slowly went into his dribble, and Derek stayed right with him, stride for stride. Once inside the foul line, Jones accelerated, took to the air—then looked as if he were about to dish to Dee Francis, the Eagles' other forward. Derek fell for the fake and moved to intercept the pass.

But while still in the air, Sky pulled the ball back and managed to toss it up underhand, over the front rim—and in!

Unbelievable! Jo marveled. Her teammate, Derek Roberts, was considered the best all-around player in the Danville County Basketball League. He could shoot, dribble, pass, rebound, defend . . . and he seldom made mistakes. But the flashiest, most exciting player in the league? *Has to be Sky Jones,* Jo thought.

Sky's basket cut the Bulls' third-quarter lead to 39–35. Dave brought the ball up for the Bulls, delivering a bounce pass to Jo after crossing midcourt. Jo stood near the right sideline, holding the ball over her head with two hands. The gym in the Essex Community Center had no bleachers, and the spectators sat in folding chairs right alongside the court. Jo was momentarily distracted by a noisy Eagles fan, but then she caught a flash of eye contact from Derek over on the right wing and knew exactly what he was going to do.

Derek started to drift away from the basket, and Sky moved with him. Then the Bulls' forward made a quick change of direction, cutting hard to the hoop. The V-cut left Sky hopelessly off balance. As Derek flashed through the lane, Jo hit him with a sharp chest pass. Derek scored the layup easily.

The Bulls' slender forward didn't raise his fist or celebrate his basket in any way. That wasn't his style. But Jo knew how seriously Derek took his competition with Sky, and how good he must have felt when he got him back.

With the Bulls ahead 41–35, Sean McClain, the Eagles' catlike point guard, again got the ball to Sky Jones. This time, without hesitation, Sky squared up and fired from outside the three-point arc.

NOTHING BUT NET

The referee threw both arms up in the air, signaling the three-point goal. Sky had sliced the Bulls' lead to 41–38.

Man, I don't envy Derek for having to guard Sky, Jo thought. *The guy just has so many weapons!*

Jo knew it was time for the Bulls to make their move. The third quarter was winding down, and Essex was behind by only three. She noticed the Eagles had shifted into a zone defense. The Bulls would need sharp ball movement to beat the zone.

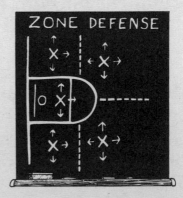

Dave brought the ball across midcourt and passed

crisply to Brian in the left corner, who immediately hit Will in the paint with a bounce pass. Jo was open just to the right of the foul line, and she put her arm up. Will, seeing her, instantly fired a two-hand over-the-head pass. Jo launched her jumper from fifteen feet.

Perfect!

Jo's hoop built the lead back to five. Sky Jones tried to answer immediately with a head-down drive to the hoop, but Will helped Derek out on defense, and Sky was forced into a wild, off-balance fling. Brian grabbed the rebound for the Bulls.

Sky may be good at a lot of things, Jo thought, *but one thing he's not good at is getting his teammates involved in the game. He's just a one-man team—and no one-man team is going to beat the Bulls!*

*   *   *

Jo and her team-mates tromped over to the Bowman's Market van, which was parked outside  the Essex Community Center. Nate's dad, Nathaniel Bowman, Sr., was the owner of Bowman's Market, where the Bulls gathered for sodas after every game and every practice. He let his son use the van, known as the Bullsmobile, to take the Bulls to and from their Saturday games.

"Hey, look who's coming along with us," Brian said to Jo sarcastically as he slid back the door on the side of the van. "Thought you'd probably have to rush back to Sampton to get to a rehearsal."

Jo had been waiting for this reaction. She was surprised only that Brian had held off for so long. Before the game, when Jim had included Jo in the starting lineup, Chunky had said, "I *knew* it!"—and had glanced over at Brian and Will with a meaningful look. She had understood exactly what the look meant. Jo had needed to miss three practices that week because of play rehearsals. Obviously a number of the Bulls had been talking about whether she'd be starting after all those absences.

And even though the Bulls had polished off the Eagles 55–43, pulling away in the fourth quarter, the grumbling about Jo's start had continued.

Jo looked Brian in the eye. "If you don't want me here, I'll find another way to get home," she said, starting to back away from the van. Balancing long play rehearsals with Bulls practices and games had made her edgy. She was in no mood for squawking from Brian or anyone else.

"Hey, lighten up, everyone," Dave said, tossing his long blond hair out of his eyes. "We won. Let's go celebrate."

"Sounds good to me," Mark added, putting a hand on Jo's shoulder and guiding her back to the van.

Jo hesitated for a second, then climbed into the Bullsmobile with the rest of the team, giving Dave and Mark a quick nod of thanks. Dave slid the door shut. Brian shot Dave and Mark a frosty look.

Jim, who'd tried to ignore the squabbling prior to the game, now looked straight at Brian and asked, "All right, what's going on here?"

Brian glared right back at the coach without answering.

But Chunky didn't hesitate to jump in. "The rule's always been no practice, no start, Coach. Why didn't that rule apply today?" he challenged. Chunky had gotten the chance to start a few games recently, and apparently, Jo realized, he'd liked it.

Jim was speechless for a moment. Nate swiveled around in the driver's seat, looking back at Chunky and the rest of the Bulls. "That rule is meant for guys who just don't show up, with no excuse," he explained, helping Jim out. "This is a different situation. Jo's told us in advance when her play rehearsals are and when she'll have to miss practice. They're excused absences."

The pudgy backup center wasn't satisfied. "You and Jim always said no exceptions," he countered, his lower lip jutting out in a pout.

Chunky's behavior reminded Jo of a dog who'd latched onto a bone and wasn't about to let it go. She was beginning to wish she were anywhere but there in the van with her teammates.

She noticed Will, who was sitting on her right, shaking his head. He wore a superior look on his face.

"Yeah, *what?*" she couldn't resist asking Will.

"I don't get it," Will said, facing her. "I mean, I could see missing a practice to go to a Chicago Bulls game or something. But to rehearse for the *school play?* Man, I'd rather have to stay after for *detention*."

Brian and Chunky laughed loudly at Will's remark. But Dave gave Jo a sympathetic look that seemed to say,

Stick to your guns. You're doing the right thing.

Jo shook her head. *This* was a switch! Just last summer, Dave had been dead set against a girl trying out for the Bulls, and Will and Brian had been her strongest allies. Now Dave was fine with her missing practices for rehearsals, and Will and Brian were bent out of shape. And Mark, the guy whose starting job she'd won, had no problems with her—but it was Chunky who was all upset.

Sometimes Jo thought she'd *never* figure these Bulls out. And she was beginning to wonder if it was worth the trouble.

CHAPTER 4

Jo gave the ball a backward spin in her hands, sighted the rim, and flexed her knees. Then she uncoiled her body, pushed her arms forward, and let fly.

Ping!

The ball nicked the front of the rim, bounced once on the asphalt, then got stuck in one of the bushes that lined the Meyersons' driveway.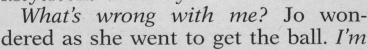

What's wrong with me? Jo wondered as she went to get the ball. *I'm usually one of the best free-throw shooters on the team!*

Not today, though. Her last miss made her two for seven.

Jo returned to the white line her father had painted on the driveway fifteen feet from the hoop and got ready to try again. This time her shot fell short—*way* short.

"Air ball!" she heard a taunting voice sing out. It was her brother, Otto. He bounded out of the house, letting the screen door slam behind him, and scooped up the ball.

Just what I need! Jo thought.

She'd had a lot on her mind even before she'd come out to shoot. Play rehearsal had run extremely long, preventing her from making it over to the Bulls' practice at Jefferson Park. She knew her teammates would be angry. As a matter of fact, she was working on her free-throw shooting partially out of sheer guilt. On top of all that, she had at least two or three hours of homework to do.

"More legs, little sister. It's all in the legs."

Jo couldn't believe her ears. Was her brother actually giving her serious advice? And not making fun of her?

Otto too was an excellent free-throw shooter—even better than Jo. And she knew he was right: When you got tired, you stopped using your legs—and that's when your shots would start to fall short.

Otto passed the ball to Jo, who hadn't moved from the white line. This time she got into a much deeper crouch before springing up and releasing the ball.

"There you go!" Otto cheered. Then, as if embarrassed at having appeared too enthusiastic, he added, "I'm amazed you can get any strength at all out of those little chicken legs of yours."

Jo looked down. She had to admit her legs *were* on the skinny side. "These little chicken legs got us eleven points against Essex last week," she responded proudly.

"Well, whoop-de-doo," Otto replied. "You got eleven points *once*. I *average* sixteen points per game." His normal swaggering tone had returned to his voice.

Putting me down, bragging about himself—this is more like the real Otto, Jo thought with a chuckle.

"Gee, I haven't heard about your sixteen-points-a-game average for at least half an hour," she replied sarcastically. "I kind of missed it."

Jo got ready to shoot again, but as she studied the basket she heard the screech of bike tires braking on pavement. Looking up, she saw that

Will, Brian, and Dave had just pulled into her driveway.

Otto dropped down on his knees on the asphalt, bowing and touching the ground with his hands repeatedly. In his most sarcastic voice, he asked, "To what do we owe this visit, O mighty Bulls? We are not worthy." Then he continued to bow in their direction a few more times.

Jo had to shake her head at how ridiculous her brother was acting, but she was also wondering what had brought the Bulls to her driveway. Jo was the only out-of-towner on the team, and the Bulls always expected her to meet them at Jefferson Park. They hardly *ever* came over to her house, even though Sampton and Branford were neighboring towns.

Something must be up, Jo sensed.

"I thought this was one of the days you were supposed to be at our practice," Will started in without beating around the bush. "The coaches were counting on you."

Jo didn't like the way Will and Brian were looking at her. She spun the basketball on her right index finger, trying to strike a casual pose.

"Rehearsal ran late," she said. "Nothing I could do about it." Seeing that Will was expecting more of an answer than that, she added, "I couldn't leave in the middle of a scene, could I?"

Brian stood straddled over the crossbar of his bike with a belligerent look on his face. "If rehearsals run so late all the time," he challenged, "why don't you skip *them* once in a while?"

"Are you *kidding?*" Jo screeched. "I can't do that. I'd be kicked right out of the play!"

Brian just stared back at her, a nasty smile creeping across his face. Jo knew what he was thinking: *Miss enough practices, and you could be kicked off the Bulls too!*

For a while nobody spoke. Jo snapped her gum loudly. She looked at Dave. Though Dave and Brian were best friends, Dave hadn't said anything in support of Brian or Will. In fact, he hadn't said anything at all. *Pretty unusual for Dave,* Jo thought.

Finally Otto yawned loudly, breaking the silence.

Will glared at Otto and then turned to Jo. "There's something else we came to tell you about," Will said. "We found a note taped to the pole on the blacktop at Jefferson. It said, 'If Jo wants to play basketball and also be in the play, then let her. There's nothing wrong with doing both.'" He stared straight into Jo's eyes. "This is the second time this week we found a note like that," he added.

"And I'll bet you have *no idea* who's been leaving us those notes, right, Jo?" Brian asked pointedly.

It was obvious to Jo what Brian was insinuating: that she was leaving the notes on her own behalf.

Jo looked Brian right in the eye. "You're right," she answered evenly. "I *don't* have any idea who's been leaving those notes."

She saw Brian and Will exchange a knowing look. Clearly they didn't believe her.

Suddenly Jo slammed the ball down on the driveway. "You guys can think whatever you want!" she yelled at them. "I don't know why you even bothered riding over here!"

She turned her back on them and returned to the white line. She got ready to shoot, pretending they were no longer there.

But it was awfully hard to concentrate. Jo knew that the four boys—Brian, Will, Dave, and Otto—were all staring at her.

And she was also trying to figure out who really *was* leaving those notes at Jefferson Park.

She lofted up the shot. The ball bounced off the left side of the rim, then landed on the driveway with a dull thud.

CHAPTER 5

Jo did her best to hurry over to her mom's blue station wagon, which was difficult, considering the load she was hauling. In her left hand was her gym duffel bag with the gear she needed for the Bulls-Ravens game. In her right hand was a heavy bag of props she'd told Ms. Sorensen, the play director, that she'd repair before the next rehearsal. She held her copy of the script between her teeth.

"Come on, Mom, fast!" she yelled as she dumped everything into the car.

"Not even hello?" Mrs. Meyerson

asked as she helped Jo with her things.

Jo didn't pick up on her mother's remark. She was too busy scrambling into the backseat so she could change into her Bulls uniform without wasting another valuable minute.

As she slipped her red-and-black number-six jersey over the T-shirt she was already wearing, Jo calculated how much time she had. The game was scheduled to start at four, and maybe it would start fifteen minutes late, if she was lucky. It was four-fifteen now. Her mom, not the world's fastest driver, could probably make it from Sampton to Rochester in half an hour. That would make it four-forty-five. . . .

She gave up trying to figure and closed her eyes for a while. Any way she looked at it, she'd miss most of the game.

And it was an important one. After dropping their first two games of the new season, the Bulls had won their next two. A win today over the weak Ravens would give them their third straight win and put them over .500.

Jo had told Jim and Nate she'd probably miss the opening tip but would be there for the majority of the game. She popped open her eyes and glanced out the window. Jo saw with satisfaction that they'd already driven out of Sampton and through Winsted. They just had to get through Harrison, then Rochester. Her eye lit on the digital clock on the dashboard. *Four-thirty already! We'll be lucky to get there before the game is over!* she fretted.

Why did rehearsal have to run so long? she asked herself. As the actual performances drew near, the rehearsals seemed to be lasting longer and longer. And today's had been a disaster!

Once Jo had noticed the rehearsal was running behind schedule and had realized she might be late for the game, she began checking the clock every three minutes. Then she started to bungle her lines. Duncan Gaines, her costar—who *was* pretty cute, she had to admit—had made fun of her.

And Ms. Sorensen had asked her to get her head out of the clouds.

Now, on top of all that, it looked as though she was going to miss most of the game anyway!

Jo clambered over the seat to join her mother up front.

"Can't you drive any faster?" she pleaded.

"I'm going as fast as I can," her mother replied. "You don't want me to get a speeding ticket, do you?"

"It wouldn't kill you!" Jo shot back.

Her mother looked at her sharply, and Jo immediately regretted her outburst. She normally wasn't rude to her parents. That was Otto's department.

"I'm sorry, Mom," Jo said. "I—I just want to get there!"

"Jo, no game is important enough to make you this upset," Mrs. Meyerson said. "Maybe you ought to just take a break from the Bulls until the play is over."

Jo was glad she hadn't told her mom about the grief some of the Bulls had given her about missing practices and games. She knew how proud her mother was about her having the lead role in the school play. If Mrs. Meyerson knew her teammates were putting pressure on her to play basketball instead of act, she might just butt in and try to straighten things out.

And as distracted as Jo was, she wasn't quite ready for that kind of embarrassment.

The Rochester gym was one of the oldest and smallest in the league. There wasn't even an electronic scoreboard. The quarter and the score were kept on number cards that were flipped over by hand, and the small timer that sat on the scorer's table was barely visible from the visitors' bench.

Jo could make out that it was the fourth quarter and that the score was Home 42, Visitors 37, but she couldn't see how much time was left on the little clock as she hurried over to join her team.

43

MJ gave Jo a welcoming nod as she slid onto the Bulls' bench, but he was the only one to greet her. Chunky deliberately looked the other way. And both coaches seemed too wrapped up in the game to notice her.

"Just over three minutes left," MJ said as he saw Jo straining to get a good look at the timer. "We've been behind most of the game," he added.

As MJ spoke, Hector Reynoso, a Ravens guard who was driving against Mark, pulled up and hit a fifteen-footer, putting Rochester ahead 44–37.

MJ shook his head. "He's been doing that all game," the Bulls' studious sub observed. "He must have fifteen points already. I don't know why Mark doesn't play him tighter."

Because Mark's not a very good defender, that's why! Jo replied silently. *If I'd been here, I could have held that guy in check.* MJ's report that Reynoso, the man Jo would have been covering, was doing most of the damage for the Ravens only made her feel *more* guilty.

Jim signaled for a time-out after Reynoso's basket, and the Bulls trooped over to their bench, heads down. Brian noticed Jo for the first time and gave her a dirty look. "Guess you missed the opening tip all right," he said sarcastically.

"I'm here now," she responded, her mouth dry.

Ignoring her response, Jim instructed, "Let's work for good shots. We're down by seven, and there's only three minutes left. We can get back into this thing, but we've got to make every possession count."

"And we need to control the boards," Nate added in his husky voice. Pounding his fist for emphasis, he chanted, "Rebound, rebound, rebound!"

The same five Bulls took the floor. Jo felt stung that the coaches hadn't thought to put her in the game. In fact, they'd hardly seemed to notice she was there!

Just as Jo was beginning to feel really sorry for herself, Nate placed a huge hand on her shoulder and said, "Hey, Jo, how'd rehearsal go today?"

"Fine," Jo answered automatically, surprised by the question. "*Long!*" she added, more accurately.

"Well, I just wanted to let you know that Jim didn't think it was a good idea to stick you in cold for these last couple of minutes," Nate offered by way of explanation.

The fact that Nate took the time to talk to her made Jo feel a little better, though she still suspected that Jim's keeping her out was a reprimand for all her no-shows and latenesses.

Derek hit a jumper on a beautiful no-look pass from Dave right after the time-out. Then Rowdy Rollins, the Ravens' bowlegged small forward, blew an easy layup. The Bulls were down by only five with two minutes still to play, and they had the ball.

But Will had a jump shot blocked by Spuds Marinaro, the Ravens' center and best player, and the Ravens recovered the ball. Five seconds later Rollins connected on a wild, spinning one-hander—and the Ravens' lead was back to seven.

Jo tried to cheer for her teammates and stay focused on the game, but it wasn't easy. Being scolded at rehearsal, rushing madly to get to the game, arriving late, being snubbed by her teammates, sitting on the bench—she just wasn't used to these things. The events of the afternoon had given her an uneasy feeling in the pit of her stomach.

On the Bulls' last few trips down the court, Dave and Mark took turns hoisting up three-point bombs in a desperate effort to catch up, but the shots weren't even close.

The final buzzer sounded. Branford had lost to Rochester, 46–39. The once-mighty Bulls, at two and three, were now *under* .500!

Jim and Nate had a lot to say to the Bulls following the defeat, but Jo wasn't able to absorb any of it. She *did*, however, hear Brian's pointed remark as the team headed for the exit. "Hey, what can you say?" the Bulls' forward began. "We were one shooting guard short of a win." Then, looking straight at Jo, he added, "Isn't that right, *Annie?*"

Jo felt like her head was spinning. She felt angry, resentful, guilty—and confused. Jo thought back to her mother's suggestion that she take a break from the Bulls until her play was over.

The way I feel right now, Jo thought bitterly, *I'd be happy to take a break from the Bulls* for good!

CHAPTER

6

"The Bulls lost—to the *Ravens?*" Mr. Bowman asked in disbelief as Jo and her teammates filed into Bowman's Market for their post-game sodas.

Jo couldn't blame Mr. Bowman for being surprised. Though the roly-poly shopkeeper could seldom make it to their games because he had to mind the store, he was still one of their most loyal fans. He got most of his information by pumping the Bulls for details as they downed their drinks at his shop. And he knew the Rochester Ravens were *not* a team that should have given the Bulls any trouble.

Most of the Bulls plopped down on stools at the counter. Jo seated herself at one of the booths. She wanted to be as far from Brian as possible. Actually, she wanted to be as far from the *whole team* as possible!

"I thought you guys were heading into this game on a winning streak," the balding Mr. Bowman continued as he handed out cold cans of Pepsi. Looking at Will, he asked, "So what happened, Too-Tall? I need the play-by-play."

Will, who was sitting on the middle stool, raised his dark eyebrows and drew in a deep breath. "They got off to a quick start, and we couldn't seem to catch 'em," he reported. "That guard named Reynoso was just a step too quick for our man Mark today," he added, clapping Mark on the shoulder consolingly.

Mark took the comment with a helpless shrug and a smile.

"We were also a little short on bench strength," Will added, swiveling around on his stool and looking pointedly at Jo, who sat alone in her booth.

Jo stared right back at him. *If you only knew what I went through to get there at all,* she thought resentfully.

"Hey, it wasn't all Reynoso," Dave offered. He was sitting on the stool next to Will. "They just outplayed us today. It didn't really matter *who* we had on the floor, or on the bench." He shot a quick, sympathetic look over to Jo.

Jo returned his look with a thankful half smile.

"Well, if you guys are heading to the NBA, as you all seem to think," Mr. Bowman kidded, "you better start getting your act together."

"Who said anything about the NBA?" Brian asked with a sly grin and a sidelong glance back at the booth where Jo was sitting. "*Some* of us obviously are more interesting in heading to *Broadway!*"

Chunky, picking up on Brian's lead, slid off his stool and made a big show of brandishing an imaginary rifle. "I can do anything better than you!" he began singing, horribly off-key.

Brian then jumped off his stool and aimed his own imaginary shotgun in retaliation. "No you can't!" He sang the answering lyric back in a mocking tone.

All the Bulls laughed.

"Well, I can understand why Jo would rather hang out with those actors than with us," Will chortled, getting in on the act. "That Duncan Gaines *is* a little better-looking than *you* are, Brian!" Then he spun around on his stool to face Jo. "Isn't that right, Annie?" he asked with a wink.

Jo felt her face turn red. She began to clench her fists. *How do these guys know about Duncan? Must have been Otto, blabbing as usual!* Jo wasn't sure who to be more furious at—her obnoxious brother or her jerky teammates.

Mr. Bowman, who'd been quietly

listening to the fun the boys were poking at Jo, picked up a rag and began mopping up a couple of wet spots on the counter. Then he slowly worked his way over to the booth where Jo was sitting and began smoothing the rag over her tabletop.

"These guys can be a little rough on you sometimes, can't they, Jo?" the shopkeeper asked in a soft, kindly voice that couldn't be overheard by the Bulls sitting at the counter.

Jo nodded her head vigorously. She felt tears coming to her eyes at the sound of Mr. Bowman's sympathetic words, but she fought them back. She was fully aware that her tabletop didn't need any cleaning. He'd just used that as an excuse to come over and talk to her. *Mr. B. is the nicest man! Why can't the guys on the Bulls be more like him?* she thought bitterly.

Mr. Bowman looked back at the counter to be sure none of Jo's teammates was listening. "Playing Annie in your school play is really important to you, isn't it?" he continued.

Jo didn't quite trust her voice to answer yet. She just nodded.

"And you made it clear to the coaches, and to your teammates—right from the get-go—about the number of practices and games you'd be missing?" Mr. Bowman pursued.

By now Jo no longer felt as though she had to worry about crying. *"Perfectly* clear," she answered firmly, though still in a soft voice, so as not to be overheard by the Bulls at the counter.

The store owner glanced over at Jo's teammates. With a knowing look on his face, he said to her, "You know, these guys are good basketball players. And they're good kids. But you and I both know they're not the most *mature* individuals in the world."

Jo laughed in hearty agreement.

"What I want to know is," Mr. Bowman went on, "are you prepared to take the kind of kidding these wiseguys are likely to dish out—just like they've been doing today—right up until the week of your performance?"

Jo took a deep breath. She knew Mr. Bowman was right. The Bulls wouldn't let up. For whatever reason, understanding that she wanted to be in the school play was just *beyond* them.

Somehow, having Mr. Bowman on her side made all the difference. Her mood brightened. "Yeah, Mr. B.," she answered, a smile spreading across her face. "I can take it."

Mr. Bowman put his hand down to meet Jo's for a low five, the trademark gesture of the Bulls. "Then go for it," he said with a big grin. "And you can certainly count on *one* old geezer being in the audience cheering for you!"

Jo gave Mr. Bowman a grateful look for the pep talk. Then she grabbed her can of soda, bounced up from her booth, and plunked herself down on the counter stool right next to Brian.

Taking note of her, Brian swiveled around and said with a look of surprise, "Well, look who's finally joining us. It's Annie Oakley!"

"That's right," Jo replied. "Hands in the air, Mister!" She poked Brian in the stomach, using her elbow as an imaginary rifle butt. Caught by surprise, Brian doubled over.

Jo laughed. It felt good to be dishing it out for a change instead of taking it. Her spirits were lifting considerably.

Hey, my parents will be there for me at the play, Jo told herself. *So will my friends from school. And so will Mr. Bowman.* She glanced around at all the Bulls with a superior look on her face. *If my teammates don't want to be there for me, then that's* their *loss—not mine!*

CHAPTER 7

Jo whipped the ball to Dave, who waited at the top of the key. She tried to put a little something extra on her pass so that neither Nate nor Jim would be able to get their hands on it. When the Bulls' starters scrimmaged against the subs and coaches, it was always a challenge to thread the ball through Nate's long arms and Jim's quick hands.

The moment Dave received the ball from Jo, he pivoted and fired a hard chest pass to Brian in the left corner of the blacktop court. Jim and Nate had endlessly drilled into the Bulls that sharp passing would win games, and Jo thought the passing of Branford's starting five was the crispest in the league.

Catching the pass from Dave, Brian squared up and launched a fadeaway jumper—his favorite shot—over the outstretched arms of MJ. Jo could tell that Brian's shot was off target, and she crashed the boards. Mark, who was supposed to be guarding her, gave her no resistance at all.

As Jo cradled the ball after grabbing the rebound, she heard Nate's shrill whistle. The tall coach always played in these practice games with a whistle between his teeth, so he could stop the action whenever he saw something he didn't like.

"You didn't box out, Mark!" Nate boomed. "Come on, you've got to rebound, rebound, rebound!" Not boxing

out, which let your man sneak in for the rebound, was one of Nate's pet peeves.

Still, usually when Nate bawled someone out, it was with a smile on his face. But not today. Jo had noticed that both coaches had been more intense than usual during the last few practices—and it didn't surprise her. On Saturday evening the Bulls were scheduled to play the Sampton Slashers, their archrivals. And though Bulls-Slashers games were *always* an event, Jo knew the coaches felt the Bulls needed a victory on Saturday to save the season.

After the loss to Rochester on the Saturday when Jo arrived at the tail end of the game, the Bulls had finally gotten their act together and had won their last two in a row. A win against the Slashers would put them at five and three—with momentum in their favor. A loss would leave them at four and four—and pretty much out of the race.

A lot was at stake in Saturday's game against the Slashers—and the toughness of the practices the last several days had reflected that.

Why, of all days, does the main perfor-mance of the play have to be this *Saturday evening?* Jo thought miserably.

After she hauled in the rebound of Brian's missed jumper, she handed the ball off to Dave, who nonchalantly brought it upcourt for the starters. Jo, an outstanding ball handler herself, admired the way Dave dribbled. He *never* had to look at the ball. It seemed as if it were attached to his hand by a rubber band.

When Dave crossed mid-court, he passed back to Jo, who had positioned herself to the right of the foul line. As soon as she caught the ball, Jo spotted Brian wide open in the left corner. She lofted a high, lazy lob in his direction. But Nate, who'd been defending Derek, stepped into the path of the ball and intercepted the pass with his long arms.

Man, he's like an octopus! Jo thought.

Nate looked at Jo, shaking his head. "I'm surprised at you, Jo," he said. "You're one of the best passers on the team. You know better than to throw a floating pass like that over the middle." Then he put a hand on Jo's shoulder. "Try that Saturday against the Slashers, and it'll be picked off every time."

Jo felt her stomach muscles tighten and the blood rush to her face. *Could Nate and Jim have forgotten?* She'd told the coaches and her teammates a million times that she'd be missing the Slashers' game because of *Annie Get Your Gun*. But when she'd found out the coaches had her practicing with the starting unit, she'd wondered if they'd forgotten.

In an unsteady voice, Jo almost whispered to Nate, "Coach, I won't be *playing* Saturday against the Slashers, remember? The school play? This is the one game I'd told you—right from the beginning—that I'd definitely have to miss."

Nate looked at Jim. Jim nodded, biting his lip.

"My fault," Jim said softly. "She *did* tell us. I forgot." Jim was the more organized of the two coaches and was the one who usually kept track of the details.

For a while nobody spoke. Jo felt all eyes on her.

Chunky broke the silence. "Why don't you just call the director the day of the play and tell her you're sick?" Chunky suggested. "Isn't that what understudies are for?"

Chunky had a strange smile on his face, and Jo couldn't tell if he was serious or not.

Brian waved his arm at Chunky. "Forget it," he said, his voice heavy with disgust. "Obviously Jo's more interested in her acting career than in the Bulls-Slashers game." Then he added, "I don't know why she doesn't just quit the Bulls altogether." He said

it as if he were talking to himself—
but more than loud enough for everyone on the blacktop to hear.

Quit the Bulls? Jo couldn't believe
Brian had the nerve to say that. *Now
he's gone too far,* she thought with satisfaction. *Finally the other guys are
going to tell him off!* Jo was sure that
Dave, MJ, or Derek—or one of the
coaches—would step up for her and
put Brian in his place.

But nobody said anything.

At that moment Will looked over at
the basketball pole—the one at which
the starters had been shooting.
Something had caught his attention.
Everyone else's gaze followed Will's.

On the grass, just off the edge of the
blacktop, was a piece of paper with a
strip of Scotch tape attached to it.
Obviously the paper had been taped
to the pole and had fallen off.

Will walked across the blacktop and
picked up the paper. Slowly he un-
folded it, then began to read aloud.
"'Basketball isn't everything,'" he read,

furrowing his thick, dark eyebrows. "'Jo really wants to be in the play. Why don't you guys give her a break?'"

Will stopped reading, looked up, and stared directly at Jo. Jo realized that Brian was staring at her too. So were some of the others. She knew what they all were thinking: that *she* had attached the note to the pole herself.

Who could be doing this? Jo wondered. *Dave? He* has *been pretty sympathetic to me through this whole deal. Maybe Derek? He's quiet, but he's a good guy. Mr. B.? He's clearly on my side!*

As Jo racked her brain for the answer, she caught a flash of movement in the trees beyond the blacktop court. All the Bulls saw it. *Someone* was sneaking from tree to tree. Then whoever it was made a run for it, up the narrow path and out through the stone gates of Jefferson Park.

Jo thought she recognized the blue

gym shorts, the black hightops, the brown hair, and the stocky build of the boy streaking out of the park. But the yellow T-shirt made her absolutely sure. She'd seen that T-shirt at breakfast that morning.

It was her brother, Otto.

So that's *who's been leaving all those messages!* Jo realized in amazement. The surprise, on top of all the tension she'd been feeling for weeks, was suddenly too much for her. Jo burst into tears.

She turned on her teammates accusingly. "Even my crummy brother understands how important this play is to me," she sobbed. "And you guys, who are supposed to be my *friends,* don't care at all!"

Before anyone had a chance to answer, Jo grabbed her sweatshirt and her ball. *This is it!* she resolved. *I've had it with these guys—for good!* She dashed up the path to the exit, catching up with her brother on Mulberry Avenue, just outside the gates of Jefferson Park.

Jo tried for the *third* time to adjust the belt, but her skirt still kept slipping down her hips. "Either this belt is too big, or I'm too skinny!" she huffed in frustration.

Two of the boys who played Indians laughed, thinking that she was joking around. Jo glared at them. She wasn't in the mood for joking.

Jo finally yanked hard enough on the belt to make the skirt stay up. Then she began fussing with the vest she was wearing, which was suede with fringe along the bottom. The top of it was chafing the back of her neck.

"Need some help, Jo?" Jimmy Delvecchio asked. Jimmy, a stage-hand, was a short, skinny kid who had a crush on Jo.

"No, I just *hate* this outfit!" Jo answered peevishly, without even looking at Jimmy. "I *never* wear skirts and vests!" Jo had liked playing Annie a whole lot better in rehearsals, when she was able to wear her basketball shorts.

That Jimmy! Jo thought angrily. *He's always . . .* Then she stopped herself. *He's always what? Trying to help me?* Why was she so mad at him? Why was everything annoying her so much? She just had a bad feeling about the whole day—and about the upcoming performance.

On top of that, Jo had a jumpy sensation in the pit of her stomach. *Butterflies! Man, I never get butterflies before a basketball game,* she reflected. Jo hadn't been terribly nervous for the three daytime, students-only performances. But this was the Saturday night show in front of classmates, friends, parents, relatives—the whole town. This was a different story!

Jo felt a tug on her ponytail. She looked back. It was Duncan Gaines, teasing her as usual. "I can do anything better than you," he crooned, his arms extended dramatically, a smile on his face.

"No, you can't," Jo was supposed to sing back, as she always did. But instead she just gave him a blank stare. She wasn't in the mood for flirting. Her costar's calm playfulness in the face of her own nervousness bothered her. *He doesn't even look all that cute today,* she thought grumpily.

The big clock on the backstage wall caught Jo's eye. *Seven-fifteen,* she noted. *The Bulls and the Slashers will be tipping off in fifteen minutes.* Then she got angry at herself for even letting the Bulls enter her mind—since she'd resolved to quit the team the day she ran out of Jefferson Park.

They're not even worth thinking about, she fumed, feeling her temperature rise. *All those nitwits care about is basketball. They've already shown me what kind of friends they are. It wouldn't bother me if I never saw any of them again!*

"Jo, you've got to help me!"

Jo was jarred out of her thoughts about the Bulls by the frantic voice of her friend Marisa, who was pulling on her sleeve. Marisa, a pretty, red-haired girl, played Dolly Tate in the show.

"I'm totally blanking out," Marisa went on, panicked. "Please run through my lines with me!"

Jo and Marisa rehearsed their scenes together. It actually made Jo feel a little better to see that someone else was more nervous than she was.

But as she spoke her lines Jo found

her thoughts drifting back to her teammates once more. Deep down, she really considered the guys on the Bulls her best friends.

How could they desert me on the biggest night of my life?

Jo blinked hard to hold back the tears.

Marisa eyed Jo curiously. "What's the matter?" she asked.

"Nothing," Jo answered. "Nothing at all!" she repeated firmly. She was determined not to let the Bulls ruin her night.

Who cares if they're not here? she said to herself. *I hope they're having a good time at their dumb basketball game!*

Jo bit her fingernails. From her position backstage, she heard the band strike up the overture. She shifted her weight nervously from one foot to the other as she waited for her cue.

She was supposed to be rehearsing

her opening scene in her head, but instead one nagging thought—*Why did I ever try out for this play?*—kept interrupting her.

What if I forget my lines and make a fool of myself in front of all these people? Jo worried as she wiped the sweat from her forehead. She hoped her makeup hadn't run. *Maybe my teammates were right in the first place. Maybe I should have just stuck to hoops!*

Her train of thought was interrupted by a gunshot. *What was that?* Jo thought, alarmed and confused.

"That's your cue!" Jimmy the stagehand said urgently, giving Jo a push. "Get going!"

Out in the center of the stage, Jo blinked several times. The lights were so bright, it seemed impossible to see. She felt as if she couldn't draw a breath. And it was incredibly *hot* up there!

Before trying to utter her first

lines, Jo peered out into the audience. She had to blink several more times, then narrow her eyes, before she could see anything. *Aha!* She spotted her parents, fifth row center, beaming broadly. Otto was sitting beside them. *Looks like Mom and Dad made him come,* she thought. *Guess he'll have to miss the Bulls-Slashers game too!*

Next she saw the proud, jovial face of Mr. Bowman, sitting in the row right behind her parents. *I knew he'd make it,* Jo thought thankfully. *You can always count on Mr. Bowman!*

She cleared her throat and was about to start speaking when her eyes were caught by the sight of a smiling face in the first row, right smack in front of her. Jo recognized the sparkling dark eyes immediately, and the fade haircut made her even more certain. It was Brian!

At first Jo couldn't believe what she was seeing. But sure enough, sitting next to Brian in the front row were

Will . . . and Dave . . . and Chunky . . . and the rest of the Bulls players and coaches!

What are they doing here? Jo thought, stunned. *They're supposed to be in Sampton, playing the Slashers!*

All at once, the Bulls held up a big white bedsheet. Painted in red on the sheet was: Break a Leg, Jo!

Jo just stared at the banner and at her teammates, her mouth hanging open.

Then a calm came over her. She stood up tall, straightened her shoulders, and smiled. And as if by magic, she *became* Annie Oakley.

CHAPTER 9

The cheering went on and on. If anything, it seemed to Jo to be getting louder! People were standing up, stomping on the floor, yelling, "Bravo! Bravo!"

Jo felt goose bumps on her skin. She couldn't believe this thunderous ovation was for her—and for her costars. Finally the curtain came down. But when it went up again, the audience was *still* cheering wildly.

The show had gone off without a hitch. Jo hadn't flubbed a single line, and she'd gotten two smaller ovations during the course of the play. The first time was when she sang "You Can't Get a Man with a Gun," and the second was later, toward the end, when she belted out "There's No Business Like Show Business." But those moments of appreciation were nothing compared to the thunderous applause and raucous yelling she was hearing now.

Jo bowed, and bowed again, and raised her hands in thanks—and still the shouting and whistling continued. She'd *never* been the center of attention like this before—not even when she'd hit a game-winning buzzer-beater. It was almost embarrassing!

Jo felt a lot of things all at once—elation, pride . . . and *relief!* As the applause finally began to die down, she remembered how nervous she'd been just before the curtain had gone up and how she'd thought that maybe she should have stuck to hoops.

And miss an experience like this? she reflected with a sense of accomplishment and satisfaction. *No way!*

"How could you *possibly* have remembered all that stuff without screwing up *once?*" Dave asked in disbelief. "You must have had seven thousand lines—at least!"

Jo was at the center of a crowd of admirers in the lobby just outside the school auditorium, and she didn't mind the attention one bit. The inner circle was made up mostly of the Bulls, but their celebration was continually interrupted by classmates, teachers, and parents wanting to give Jo a high five or to tell her, "Nice going." Mr. and Mrs. Meyerson had already stopped by for a big congratulatory hug and kiss, and Mr. Bowman had delivered Jo a bouquet of flowers.

Amid the hubbub, Jo tried to answer Dave's question. "Well, I don't know if it was exactly seven thousand lines," she began, "but you're right—it wasn't always easy. There were days I'd be trying to learn the words to 'I'm an Indian Too' and all I'd be able to hear in my head was Nate shouting, 'Rebound, rebound, rebound!'"

All the Bulls, Nate especially, laughed long and hard.

"I just couldn't believe the reaction we got from the audience," Jo went on enthusiastically, her eyes taking in the hordes of people still crowding the lobby. Then her face lit up as a new thought struck her. "And I can't believe you guys made it here! You really skipped your game against the Slashers just to see me?"

She saw all the Bulls looking at one another self-consciously.

Finally Mark, with a straight face, said, "Of *course* we came to see you. Did you ever really think we wouldn't?"

Jo laughed heartily at Mark's reply. The other Bulls laughed too, although somewhat sheepishly.

"I guess you had a pretty good reason to think we wouldn't show, after all that grief we gave you about missing basketball to be in the play," Will said, his eyes glued to his size-ten sneakers. Gradually he looked up at Jo. "But then Otto's notes finally made us wise up—you know, when he wrote that stuff about how there's more to life than just basketball."

"Yeah," Mark agreed, "even though he's a total sleazeball, we realized he had a point there."

Jo didn't even flinch at the dissing of her brother. All the Bulls did it constantly—and half the time Jo joined in herself.

"It took us some time," Brian added, "but after a while it dawned on us that if one of our teammates was crazy enough to star in a school play, we'd just better be there to make sure she didn't screw up."

Jo knew this was Brian's way of finally admitting he'd been wrong. For a moment she felt tears coming to her eyes. It seemed as if all her loneliness and frustration of the past month was about to burst loose. But she was determined not to let her emotions show.

"So you just blew the game off?" Jo asked as breezily as she could. "Just didn't show?"

"Well, actually," Jim began, "I was thinking of calling Coach White and asking for a postponement—"

"But we all knew that nasty old weasel would never let us off the hook," Dave jumped in, finishing Jim's sentence for him.

"Dave's right," Jim agreed. "Coach White would never have given us a break, so I didn't even bother calling him. I *did* call your brother, though, to let him know we wouldn't be at the game. Of course, we made him swear he wouldn't tell *you* we'd be here at the play tonight."

"So does that mean the Bulls had to forfeit the game?" Jo asked, feeling a little guilty.

"Hey, if the Slashers want to count it as a loss for us, then let 'em count it as a loss," Brian answered. "We'll beat 'em another time."

Jo laughed inwardly at Brian's change of heart. *A week ago, Brian would have thought of a loss to the Slashers as a major world disaster,* Jo realized.

As the conversation continued, yet another kid began squeezing his way through the circle of Bulls. Jo assumed it was another classmate offering congratulations—but she was wrong.

It was her brother, Otto.

Oh, no, what does he *want?* was Jo's first reaction.

Otto threw an arm around his sister's shoulders. Jo didn't like the sly grin he wore on his freckled face.

"Well, I've got some good news for you guys," Otto announced, looking around at Jo and the rest of the Bulls.

"Let me guess. You're moving to another state!" Dave quipped. His teammates cheered his remark.

Otto brushed aside the insult, holding up his two hands for quiet. "Now, now, guys, let's not jump to conclusions. I can be a good guy when I want to be."

Jo heard Mark and Chunky snickering.

Ignoring them, Otto plunged

ahead. "When I heard you guys were going to finally do the right thing and stand by your teammate," Otto said, "I got on the phone with our coach, Mr. White"—he glanced at Dave and flashed one of his rare smiles—"who isn't nearly the skunk you think he is. I asked him about rescheduling the game for tomorrow—"

Jo grabbed his arm. "You didn't!" she said, her eyes again filling with tears.

"Hey, I didn't just do it for *your* sake," Otto objected, pulling away from his sister's grasp. "You think I wanted to lose the chance of schooling you guys like we always do?"

Jo couldn't help smiling at her

brother. He always tried to make the Bulls think he was totally obnoxious, but every once in a while he slipped up.

"And?" Brian pursued anxiously. "What did Coach White say?"

Otto took his time answering. Jo knew he was enjoying the agony he was causing all the Bulls.

"Well?" Nate pressed in his husky voice.

Otto shrugged. "He said no problem."

At Otto's response, the Bulls began dancing around and around in a circle, with Otto and Jo caught up in the middle.

"So thanks to your old enemy," Otto said, thumping himself on the chest as the Bulls celebrated, "you not only got to see the play, but you didn't even have to miss your game."

Then, looking at Jo, he added, "And you'll have Annie Oakley on your side with that rifle of hers—shooting threes!"

Jo knew Otto would never admit it, but for a second—just for a *second*—her older brother looked as if he might be a little proud of her.

About the Author

Hank Herman is a writer and newspaper columnist who lives in Connecticut with his wife, Carol, and their three sons, Matt, Greg, and Robby.

His column, "The Home Team," appears in the *Westport News*. It's about kids, sports, and life in the suburbs.

Although Mr. Herman was formerly the editor in chief of *Health* magazine, he now writes mostly about sports. At one time, he was a tennis teacher, and he has also run the New York City Marathon. He coaches kids' basketball every winter and Little League baseball every spring.

He runs, bicycles, skis, kayaks, and plays tennis and basketball on a regular basis. Mr. Herman admits that he probably spends about as much time playing, coaching, and following sports as he does writing.

Of all sports, basketball is his favorite.

CHOOSE YOUR OWN
NIGHTMARE™

Control your fate—before it's too late!

Dare to be scared?
Evil pen pals, vicious vampires, and creepy zombies are after
you! Haunting your school, invading your favorite video
arcade—and living right next door. Every page is a terrifying
turn—and *you* decide just how scared you want to be!

Find all the spine-tingling
CHOOSE YOUR OWN NIGHTMARE
titles wherever books are sold.